A SEARCH
IS ORGANDIZED

A SEARCH
IS ORGANDIZED

A.A. MILNE

illustrated by
ERNEST H. SHEPARD

TED SMART

A SEARCH
IS ORGANDIZED

Pooh was sitting in his house one day,
counting his pots of honey, when there
came a knock on the door.

'Fourteen,' said Pooh. 'Come in.
Fourteen. Or was it fifteen? Bother.
That's muddled me.'

'Hallo, Pooh,' said Rabbit.

'Hallo, Rabbit. Fourteen, wasn't it?'

'What was?'

'My pots of honey what I was counting.'

'Fourteen, that's right.'

'Are you sure?'

'No,' said Rabbit. 'Does it matter?'

'I just like to know,' said Pooh humbly.
'So as I can say to myself: "I've got
fourteen pots of honey left." Or fifteen,
as the case may be. It's sort of
comforting.'

'Well, let's call it sixteen,' said Rabbit.
'What I came to say was: Have you seen
Small anywhere about?'

'I don't think so,' said Pooh. And then, after thinking a little more, he said: 'Who is Small?'

'One of my friends-and-relations,' said Rabbit carelessly.

This didn't help Pooh much, because Rabbit had so many friends-and-relations, and of such different sorts and sizes, that he didn't know whether he ought to be looking for Small at the top of an oak-tree or in the petal of a buttercup.

'I haven't seen anybody to-day,' said Pooh, 'not so as to say "Hallo, Small!" to. Did you want him for anything?'

'*I* don't *want* him,' said Rabbit. 'But it's always useful to know where a friend-and-relation *is*, whether you want him or whether you don't.'

'Oh, I see,' said Pooh. 'Is he lost?'

'Well,' said Rabbit, 'nobody has seen him for a long time, so I suppose he is. Anyhow,' he went on importantly, 'I

promised Christopher Robin I'd
Organize a Search for him, so come on.'

Pooh said good-bye affectionately to his
fourteen pots of honey, and hoped they
were fifteen; and he and Rabbit went out
into the Forest.

'Now,' said Rabbit, 'this is a Search, and
I've Organized it —'

'Done what to it?' said Pooh.

'Organized it. Which means — well, it's what you do to a Search, when you don't all look in the same place at once. So I want *you*, Pooh, to search by the Six Pine Trees first, and then work your way towards Owl's House, and look out for me there. Do you see?'

'No,' said Pooh. 'What —'

'Then I'll see you at Owl's House in about an hour's time.'

'Is Piglet organdized too?'

'We all are,' said Rabbit, and off he went.

As soon as Rabbit was out of sight, Pooh remembered that he had forgotten to ask who Small was, and whether he was the sort of friend-and-relation who settled on one's nose, or the sort who got trodden on by mistake, and as it was Too Late Now, he thought he would begin the Hunt by looking for Piglet, and asking him what they were looking for before he looked for it.

'And it's no good looking at the Six Pine Trees for Piglet,' said Pooh to himself, 'because he's been organdized in a special place of his own. So I shall have to look for the Special Place first. I wonder where it is.' And he wrote it down in his head like this:

ORDER OF LOOKING FOR THINGS.

1. Special Place.   *(To find Piglet.)*
2. Piglet.   *(To find who Small is.)*
3. Small.   *(To find Small.)*
4. Rabbit   *(To tell him I've found Small.)*
5. Small Again.   *(To tell him I've found Rabbit.)*

'Which makes it look like a bothering sort of day,' thought Pooh, as he stumped along.

The next moment the day became very bothering indeed, because Pooh was so busy not looking where he was going that he stepped on a piece of the Forest which had been left out by mistake; and he only just had time to think to himself: 'I'm flying. What Owl does. I wonder how you stop — ' when he stopped.

Bump!

'Ow!' squeaked something.

'That's funny,' thought Pooh. 'I said "Ow!" without really oo'ing.'

'Help!' said a small, high voice.

'That's me again,' thought Pooh. 'I've had an Accident, and fallen down a well, and my voice has gone all squeaky and works before I'm ready for it, because I've done something to myself inside. Bother!'

'Help — help!'

'There you are! I say things when I'm not trying. So it must be a very bad Accident.' And then he thought that perhaps when he did try to say things he wouldn't be able to; so, to make sure, he said loudly: 'A Very Bad Accident to Pooh Bear.'

'Pooh!' squeaked the voice.

'It's Piglet!' cried Pooh eagerly. 'Where are you?'

'Underneath,' said Piglet in an underneath sort of way.

'Underneath what?'

'You,' squeaked Piglet. 'Get up!'

'Oh!' said Pooh, and scrambled up as quickly as he could. 'Did I fall on you, Piglet?'

'You fell on me,' said Piglet, feeling himself all over.

'I didn't mean to,' said Pooh
sorrowfully.

'I didn't mean to be underneath,' said
Piglet sadly. 'But I'm all right now, Pooh,
and I *am* so glad it was you.'

'What's happened?' said Pooh.
'Where are we?'

'I think we're in a sort of Pit. I was
walking along, looking for somebody, and
then suddenly I wasn't any more, and just
when I got up to see where I was,
something fell on me. And it was you.'

'So it was,' said Pooh.

'Yes,' said Piglet. 'Pooh,' he went on
nervously, and came a little closer, 'do you
think we're in a Trap?'

Pooh hadn't thought about it at all, but
now he nodded. For suddenly he
remembered how he and Piglet had once
made a Pooh Trap for Heffalumps, and
he guessed what had happened. He and
Piglet had fallen into a Heffalump Trap

for Poohs! That was what it was.

'What happens when the Heffalump comes?' asked Piglet trembling, when he had heard the news.

'Perhaps he won't notice *you*, Piglet,' said Pooh encouragingly, 'because you're a Very Small Animal.'

'But he'll notice *you*, Pooh.'

'He'll notice *me*, and I shall notice *him*,' said Pooh, thinking it out. 'We'll notice each other for a long time, and then he'll say: "Ho-*ho*!"'

Piglet shivered a little at the thought of that 'Ho-*ho*!' and his ears began to twitch.

'W-what will *you* say?' he asked.

Pooh tried to think of something he would say, but the more he thought, the more he felt that there *is* no real answer to 'Ho-*ho*!' said by a Heffalump in the sort of voice this Heffalump was going to say it in.

'I shan't say anything,' said Pooh at last. 'I shall just hum to myself, as if I was waiting for something.'

'Then perhaps he'll say "Ho-*ho*!" again?' suggested Piglet anxiously.

'He will,' said Pooh.

Piglet's ears twitched so quickly that he had to lean them against the side of the Trap to keep them quiet.

'He will say it again,' said Pooh, 'and I shall go on humming. And that will Upset him. Because when you say "Ho-*ho*!" twice, in a gloating sort of way, and the other person only hums, you suddenly find, just as you begin to say it the third time that — that — well, you find —'

'What?'

'That it isn't,' said Pooh.

'Isn't what?'

Pooh knew what he meant, but, being a Bear of Very Little Brain, couldn't think of the words.

'Well, it just isn't,' he said again.

'You mean it isn't ho-*ho*-ish any more?' said Piglet hopefully.

Pooh looked at him admiringly and said that that was what he meant — if you went on humming all the time, because you couldn't go on saying 'Ho-*ho*!' for *ever*.

'But he'll say something else,' said Piglet.

'That's just it. He'll say: "What's all this?" And then *I* shall say — and this is a very good idea, Piglet, which I've just thought of — *I* shall say: "It's a trap for a Heffalump which I've made, and I'm waiting for the Heffalump to fall in." And I shall go on humming. That will Unsettle him.'

'Pooh!' cried Piglet, and now it was *his* turn to be the admiring one. 'You've saved us!'

'Have I?' said Pooh, not feeling quite sure.

But Piglet was quite sure; and his mind ran on, and he saw Pooh and the Heffalump talking to each other, and he thought suddenly, and a little sadly, that it *would* have been rather nice if it had been Piglet and the Heffalump talking so grandly to each other, and not Pooh, much as he loved Pooh; because he really had more brain than Pooh, and the conversation would go better if he and not Pooh were doing one side of it, and it would be comforting afterwards in the evenings to look back on the day when he answered a Heffalump back as bravely as if the Heffalump wasn't there. It seemed so easy now. He knew just what he would say:

HEFFALUMP (*gloatingly*): 'Ho-*ho*!'
  PIGLET (*carelessly*): 'Tra-la-la, tra-la-la.'
  HEFFALUMP (*surprised, and not quite so sure of himself*): 'Ho-*ho*!'
  PIGLET (*more carelessly still*): 'Tiddle-um-tum, tiddle-um-tum.'
  HEFFALUMP (*beginning to say Ho-ho and turning it awkwardly into a cough*): 'H'r'm! What's all this?'
  PIGLET (*surprised*): 'Hallo! This is a trap I've made, and I'm waiting for a Heffalump to fall into it.'

HEFFALUMP *(greatly disappointed)*: 'Oh!'
(After a long silence): 'Are you sure?'

PIGLET: 'Yes.'

HEFFALUMP: 'Oh!' *(nervously)*: 'I — I
thought it was a trap *I'd* made to catch
Piglets.'

PIGLET *(surprised)*: 'Oh, no!'

HEFFALUMP: 'Oh!' *(apologetically)*: 'I — I
must have got it wrong, then.'

PIGLET: 'I'm afraid so.' *(politely)*: 'I'm
sorry.' *(He goes on humming.)*

HEFFALUMP: 'Well — well — I — well.
I suppose I'd better be getting back?'

PIGLET *(looking up carelessly)*: 'Must you? Well, if you see Christopher Robin anywhere, you might tell him I want him.'

HEFFALUMP *(eager to please)*: 'Certainly! Certainly!' *(He hurries off.)*

POOH *(who wasn't going to be there, but we find we can't do without him)*: 'Oh, Piglet, how brave and clever you are!'

PIGLET *(modestly)*: 'Not at all, Pooh.' *(And then, when Christopher Robin comes, Pooh can tell him all about it.)*

While Piglet was dreaming his happy dream, and Pooh was wondering again whether it was fourteen or fifteen, the Search for Small was still going on all over the Forest. Small's real name was Very Small Beetle, but he was called Small for short, when he was spoken to at all, which hardly ever happened except when somebody said: '*Really*, Small!' He had been staying with Christopher Robin for a

few seconds, and he had started round a gorse-bush for exercise, but instead of coming back the other way, as expected, he hadn't, so nobody knew where he was.

'I expect he's just gone home,' said Christopher Robin to Rabbit.

'Did he say Good-bye-and-thank-you-for-a-nice-time?' said Rabbit.

'He's only just said how-do-you-do,' said Christopher Robin.

'Ha!' said Rabbit. After thinking a little, he went on: 'Has he written a letter saying how much he enjoyed himself, and how sorry he was he had to go so suddenly?'

Christopher Robin didn't think he had.

'Ha!' said Rabbit again, and looked very important. 'This is Serious. He is Lost. We must begin the Search at once.'

Christopher Robin, who was thinking of something else, said: 'Where's Pooh?' — but Rabbit had gone. So he went into his house and drew a picture of Pooh going a long walk at about seven o'clock in the morning, and then he climbed to the top of his tree and climbed down again, and then he wondered what Pooh was doing, and went across the Forest to see.

It was not long before he came to the Gravel Pit, and he looked down, and there were Pooh and Piglet, with their backs to him, dreaming happily.

'Ho-*ho*!' said Christopher Robin loudly and suddenly.

Piglet jumped six inches in the air with Surprise and Anxiety, but Pooh went on dreaming.

'It's the Heffalump!' thought Piglet nervously. 'Now, then!' He hummed in his throat a little, so that none of the words should stick, and then, in the most delightfully easy way, he said: 'Tra-la-la, tra-la-la,' as if he had just thought of it. But he didn't look round, because if you look round and see a Very Fierce Heffalump looking down at you, sometimes you forget what you were going to say.

'Rum-tum-tum-tiddle-um,' said Christopher Robin in a voice like Pooh's. Because Pooh had once invented a song which went:

Tra-la-la, tra-la-la,
Tra-la-la, tra-la-la,
Rum-tum-tum-tiddle-um.

So whenever Christopher Robin sings it, he always sings it in a Pooh-voice, which seems to suit it better.

'He's said the wrong thing,' thought Piglet anxiously. 'He ought to have said, "Ho-*ho*!" again. Perhaps I had better say it for him.' And, as fiercely as he could, Piglet said: 'Ho-*ho*!'

'How *did* you get there, Piglet?' said Christopher Robin in his ordinary voice.

'This is Terrible,' thought Piglet. 'First he talks in Pooh's voice, and then he talks in Christopher Robin's voice, and he's doing it so as to Unsettle me.' And being now Completely Unsettled, he said very quickly and squeakily: 'This is a trap for Poohs, and I'm waiting to fall in it, ho-*ho*, what's all this, and then I say ho-*ho* again.'

'*What?*' said Christopher Robin.

'A trap for ho-ho's,' said Piglet huskily. 'I've just made it, and I'm waiting for the ho-ho to come-come.'

How long Piglet would have gone on like this I don't know, but at that moment Pooh woke up suddenly and decided that it was sixteen. So he got up; and as he turned his head so as to soothe himself in that awkward place in the middle of the back where something was tickling him, he saw Christopher Robin.

'Hallo!' he shouted joyfully.

'Hallo, Pooh.'

Piglet looked up, and looked away again. And he felt so Foolish and Uncomfortable that he had almost decided to run away to Sea and be a Sailor, when suddenly he saw something.

'Pooh!' he cried. 'There's something climbing up your back.'

'I thought there was,' said Pooh.

'It's Small!' cried Piglet.

'Oh, *that's* who it is, is it?' said Pooh.

'Christopher Robin, I've found Small!' cried Piglet.

'Well done, Piglet,' said Christopher Robin.

And at these encouraging words Piglet felt quite happy again, and decided not to be a Sailor after all. So when Christopher Robin had helped them out of the Gravel Pit, they all went off together hand-in-hand.

And two days later Rabbit happened to meet Eeyore in the Forest.

'Hallo, Eeyore,' he said, 'what are *you* looking for?'

'Small, of course,' said Eeyore. 'Haven't you any brain?'

'Oh, but didn't I tell you?' said Rabbit. 'Small was found two days ago.'

There was a moment's silence.

'Ha-ha,' said Eeyore bitterly. 'Merriment and what-not. Don't apologize. It's just what *would* happen.'

A Search is Organdized
is taken from *The House at Pooh Corner*
originally published in Great Britain 11th October 1928
by Methuen & Co. Ltd.
Text by A.A.Milne and line drawings by Ernest H.Shepard
copyright under the Berne Convention

First published 1991 by Methuen Children's Books
an imprint of Egmont Children's Books Limited
239 Kensington High Street, London W8 6SA

This edition first produced in 1998 for The Book People
Hall Wood Avenue, Haydock, St Helens WA11 9UL

ISBN 1 85613 489 X

3 5 7 9 10 8 6 4

Printed in Hong Kong

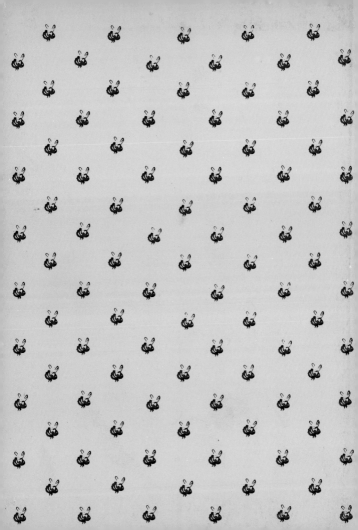